CH00802585

The Godmother

Cathy Cade

Copyright © 2020 Cathy Cade

All rights reserved.

ISBN: 978-1-9163127-5-3

CONTENTS

TO PICKLE

Wherever she is now

i

1 The Godmother

Euphemia Ffinch focused on her target, knowing she must shoot quickly. Her quarry had taken cover in the acacia but might be off again at any moment.

Her hand was steady as she adjusted her aim… and shot.

Satisfied, she relaxed back into the one comfortable chair on the wooden veranda and replaced the camera on the low table beside her.

Picking up the gilt-edged card that lay there, she re-read the invitation. It had arrived today from a former life lived by a different Euphemia. Memories flowed back.

Memories of the palace where she had been nanny to the little prince and princess of Regalia.

Memories of her cousin Bertie and Lucinda Eleanor, the goddaughter she had not seen since her cousin remarried.

Memories of a different world.

When she raised her eyes again, the sun was touching the horizon. Trees darkened against a tangerine sky and lights flickered behind her.

Across the compound, lights blinked on above the door of each dormitory and windows glowed bright. The song of reed-frogs replaced the song of the bird in the acacia tree.

She fancied the wee birdie with the big voice might be a cousin of the one that sang to her from the roof of the Emir's palace as she left Djalladin last month. The memory of that drive kindled a premonition that she would not see her old friend, the Emir, again.

Yet the orphanage here had needed her help. An email from its supervisor had set her intuition prickling, and her intuition had been right. It usually was.

Now that threat was removed, but a sense of foreboding still shadowed her. She didn't think it came from Djalladin.

Trouble loomed back home. She just didn't know what it was, yet.

2 The Uglies

The heavy doorknocker hammered against thick oak, echoing around the panelled entrance hall. Buttons raced up the basement stairs with a warning bark.

But it was only the postman. He handed an oversized envelope to the Baroness and bent to scratch behind Buttons' ear. 'Hello old boy.'

'Ah, the Royal Seal,' announced Baroness Fincham, as if she regularly received letters from the palace.

'They all 'ave,' said the postman. 'It's yer invitation to the royal ball.'

Buttons imagined a royal ball would be a big golden one. It must be enormous if they were inviting lots of people to play with it.

The Baroness shoved him aside with her foot and closed the door.

At the mention of a ball, her three daughters gathered in the hallway while the Baroness tore at the envelope. A rare smile disturbed the careful make-up that recalled her former beauty.

Her daughters took after their father.

As she opened the perfumed envelope, she sneezed.

'I think I'm becoming allergic to dogs.'

She glared at Buttons as she unfolded the gilt-edged invitation and began to read.

'The Hon Baroness Fincham, Miss Tabitha Uglie, Miss Abigail… blah, blah… cordially invited to a ball to celebrate Prince Alfred's birthday.'

Her daughters' squeals drowned the rest of the words.

'Shh!' Their mother's eyes flicked towards the basement. 'At least try to *behave* like ladies.'

'Princess Aureila will hardly be back from her honeymoon by then,' said Harriet. She was the youngest and the tallest of the sisters. 'Her wedding isn't till the week after next.'

'All good for tourism,' murmured the Baroness who had shares in several hotels.

She raised the spectacles that hung from a gold chain around her neck and inspected her three daughters.

'The Prince must find a wife,' she said, 'and there aren't many princesses around these days.'

She sighed before letting the spectacles fall.

Abigail, the heaviest of the sisters, jostled to see the invitation and trod on Buttons' tail. He pulled it free, leaving behind a chunk of white fur.

Tabitha, the eldest sister, snatched the card from her mother's hand.

'Look, our names are all in posh curly writing: Miss Tabitha Uglie, Miss Abigail Uglie, Miss Harriet Uglie, The Honourable Lucinda Eleanor Fincham–'

'*Cinders*?' Abigail honked.

Her mother glowered at the basement stairs.

'Shh! Keep your voice down.' She folded the invitation. 'There won't be room in the taxi; they're only insured for four passengers.'

She slipped the card back into its envelope. 'Anyway, she doesn't have anything suitable to wear.'

'But, *my* ballgown isn't–'

'I'll need–'

Buttons barked, and Abigail aimed a kick at him. He dodged the silly goose and ran down to the basement.

An unpleasant chemical smell drifted up the stairs to greet him. He found his Mistress kneeling on the stone floor, in front of the oven. She pushed back her brown fringe with the back of her wrist, adding another smudge to her forehead.

Her eyes looked tired this close up. He barked his news at her.

'Don't worry, Buttons. I haven't forgotten your walk – as soon as I've finished cleaning the oven.'

His Master had never understood him either, although it didn't seem to matter back then. He curled up in his corner on Master's cardigan.

This wasn't the cardigan he'd chewed the buttons off when he first came – the one that earned him his name. That cardigan fell apart years ago.

He had been a different dog back then. Now he had responsibilities.

Mistress gave him this cardigan after the Master died but it no longer smelled of him. All Buttons had left of Master was his daughter, Cindy – Buttons' Mistress.

Buttons and Mistress had the house to themselves after their walk; everyone else had gone out. He had heard the front door slam and the house relaxed, creaking and sighing in the silence. Mistress went to make the beds.

Afterwards he snoozed at her feet while she examined a laptop she'd found in a wastebasket upstairs.

Woken by the slam of the front door, he raised an eyelid in time to see the tail of a mouse disappear into the under-stairs cupboard.

The Baroness called down for coffee and biscuits.

'They've been shopping for ballgowns,' Mistress told him on her return from delivering the coffee. 'They're going to the Prince's birthday ball.'

Buttons wasn't sure what a birthday was, but he tried again to tell Mistress she'd been invited to play with this ball, barking three times and wagging his tail.

'Yes, boy. Anyone would think you understood every word.' She poured a coffee for herself. 'We'll have the house to ourselves that evening. There might be something worth watching on TV.'

He whined.

Harriet, the youngest of the stepsisters, came down with a glove in need of stitching.

When the Uglie family first came to Fincham House, Buttons saw the older sisters pinching and poking Harriet when the grown-ups weren't around. They'd call her names like 'lamp-post' and 'maypole.'

Since Master died, they bullied Mistress instead and Harriet had stayed out of the way, glad not to be the focus of their attention.

Mistress opened her sewing box and nodded towards the laptop on the table.

'Did Tabitha mean to throw this laptop away?' she asked. 'It seems to be working.'

'She said the webcam were broke,' said Harriet, 'and the microphone. Ma's bought her a new one.'

'Would they mind me using this, then?'

'Nah.' Harriet scratched her head. 'That is… she'd probably want something for it,' Tabitha was greedy as a gull, and twice as vicious, 'but I won't tell.'

Cindy thanked her with a smile, and Buttons wagged his tail so hard his body waggled. Harriet stroked his back and spoke with her head down.

'Ma reckons she's become allergic to dogs. She's hinting about getting rid of Buttons.'

She sneaked a look at Mistress, whose face was expressionless as she stitched.

'Ma reckons he's too old and too slow to catch mice.'

Mistress held out the mended glove by its little finger, a rare flash of spirit in her eyes. The glove dangled like a dead mouse.

'He's not hers to get rid of.'

Harriet stood. 'P-perhaps, if you keep him out of her way,' she took the glove, 'she might forget about being allergic.'

Her face red, she fled to the stairs as voices grew louder above them in the hallway.

Buttons looked up at Mistress and whined softly. It wasn't Harriet's fault. She'd only been warning them.

Harriet turned at the bottom of the stairs, her eyes apologetic and her lip trembling. Mistress managed a half-smile. It was answered by a wobbly grin.

'Ta for this,' said Harriet, and ran up the steps as if she'd said something rude.

Her sisters descended, pushing her against the stair-rail on their way past. Their voices competed for attention as they demanded alterations to their new ballgowns.

Buttons wasn't surprised to learn the Baroness wanted to get rid of him. He had never trusted her. She was careful not to show her true nature while Master was alive, but dogs are good judges of people.

Malegra Uglie had been a wealthy widow in search of a title, and the Master was penniless. She offered to buy Fincham House from him so he would have money to pay off his debts before they married.

No-one expected he would die so soon, leaving his young daughter at the mercy of her stepmother. Nor that Malegra would make her cook and clean in return for a room in the basement, so that the Baroness could dismiss the maid.

It didn't take long for the old witch to start complaining about the price of dog food.

A cotton reel rolled from the table and bounced off Buttons' head. He looked up to see if Mistress had noticed. She smiled back at him from the mound of white lace that covered her lap as she sewed more bows and flounces onto Tabitha's ballgown.

'She's going to flap like a windy washing line in this,' she told him as she stitched, 'and Abigail is going to look like an enormous yellow meringue in hers. Their mother, as always, will be resplendent in black.' She bit off a thread. 'Like a crow.'

3 Harriet

Harriet came down the stairs with an armful of dusky-pink silk.

Mistress stiffened, and Buttons nudged her hand with his nose. She looked down at him.

His eyes pleaded for Harriet and this time she seemed to understand.

'That's a nice colour,' said Mistress, grudgingly. 'What does it need?'

'I dunno.'

Harriet shrugged. 'It looked alright in the shop mirror when the salesgirl was fussing behind me, but in my bedroom mirror it looks like a mousy sack.' She sighed. 'You always look like a fashion doll, even in torn jeans and your Pa's old shirts, but I reckon it'd take a magic wand to make me look good in this.'

She threw the gown over a chair and wandered to the mantelpiece where she picked up a photograph.

'Your Ma looks like a princess in this photo. Your Pa told us she were an artist. Didn't she paint that picture of him that used to hang in the hall?'

'Try the dress on,' said Mistress. 'I'll see what I can do.'

Buttons glanced towards the under-stairs cupboard, as if the door might fall open, revealing the Master's portrait. But Mistress had concealed the painting well after the Baroness took it down. The old crow wouldn't venture in among the spider-webs.

Mistress zipped Harriet into the flowing ballgown. Its lines were simple – like a tent.

'It fits where it touches,' she said. 'I can take in the seams and add some darts.' She circled, tucking and pinning, and stood back to view the result.

'See what you think. There's a mirror in the bedroom.'

The bedroom was a converted storeroom at the back of the basement. After a few minutes, Harriet sang out from the other room. 'That's magic! Even with pins in, it looks amazing.'

Mistress watched her stepsister returning with shoulders hunched and eyes lowered.

'You won't get to look shorter by stooping,' she said as she unzipped Harriet. 'Carry your height proudly. Think "swan".'

'Me? I'm an Uglie duckling.' Harriet draped her ballgown over the back of the worn armchair. 'Ma says my face is lopsided, and my nose is too big.'

'I wouldn't say that,' said Mistress. 'It's a noble nose.'

'Don't you mean knobbly?' said Harriet, buttoning her blouse.

Mistress giggled. 'No, I don't. It's perfectly straight. What's more, it's shorter than Tabitha's and thinner than Abigail's.'

Harriet raised her head, looked down her nose and crossed her eyes.

Mistress's snort of laughter brought a smile in return. 'I don't think I've seen you laugh since your Pa died.'

Mistress stopped chuckling.

'I miss him too, you know,' said Harriet. 'He always had time for us. Not the way you must miss him, of course.' She sighed. 'Not the way I still miss my Pa – even now.' She picked up a shoe and hugged it. 'He was like a hurricane sweeping through the room and carrying everyone along with him. He made me feel special.'

Mistress smiled. 'Mine was more of a gentle breeze,' she said. 'But if something upset me, he knew how to make it seem… unimportant.'

Harriet nodded and Buttons relaxed as they all remembered the Master.

Harriet pulled the shoe on over her heel. As she raised her head her eyes went to the computer open on the table.

'How are you getting on with that laptop? Do you need any help?'

'It's magic! It shows me all the countries of the world. I'd love to travel the world for real one day. I even found a page about my godmother – she's away travelling – but I lost it when I closed the browser by mistake.'

Harriet slipped the shoe she was holding onto her foot and sat at the table.

'Let's try to find it again. If you click here, it lists all the web pages you opened before. Can you see the one you lost?'

'There, that's the one – about orphanages in Africa.' Harriet clicked on the link. 'And that's my godmother, Euphemia Ffinch. When she wasn't at Father's funeral I thought she might have died too, but she sent a card on my birthday.'

There was that word again – birthday. Buttons remembered the card arriving. She'd read it out to him, and then she'd stood it on the mantelpiece, next to the photograph, where it stayed for weeks. Birthdays must last a long time.

Harriet scrolled down the web page. 'There's a link here to her blog; you can follow that and post messages for her to read. Only be careful – everyone else can read them too.'

'That's brilliant, Harriet. Thanks for finding it.'

Buttons thumped his tail and Harriet glowed.

'Let's have a look at that webcam and microphone,' said Harriet. The laptop clicked and beeped as her fingers moved. 'I'm good at fixing things.'

A voice shrilled from upstairs. 'Are you down there, Harriet? Bring some tea and toast when you come up.'

The girls looked at each other and Harriet raised an eyebrow.

'I'll look at the laptop when I come back for the dress, shall I?'

She put the kettle on, and Mistress headed for the pantry. A mouse ran out as she opened the door.

Buttons pounced, but it scampered to safety under the door of the stair-cupboard.

As Buttons rested by Mistress's feet, daylight faded in the street outside. The sun's rays never reached the basement area where steps led down from the street to their door. Even on the brightest day, their light was poor, and the single ceiling bulb was already lit.

The bedroom had a brighter view, being tucked away by the back door which led to the south-facing garden. But Mistress didn't spend time in the bedroom during daylight hours.

She read him highlights from Aunt Phemie's blog.

Euphemia Ffinch had set out to travel the world back when Buttons was a pup and was still travelling. The words Mistress read brought to his mind the brisk person who wrote them, even though Aunt Phemie hadn't visited Regalia since Master's wedding.

Buttons recalled a round sort of person who would bounce into a room and wake it up. Her generous mouth curved upwards, as did the twinkling eyes and curling strands of escaping hair. Even her wrinkles smiled.

She had understood him. Always.

Mistress was saying, '…And here's her email address. I'm going to set up an email account so I can send her a proper message.'

It was some time later when her squeal of excitement woke him from a dream of cowering mice. Aunt Phee had replied to her email already.

Excitement soon changed to sadness.

'Oh, Buttons, she's asked how Father is. Nobody told her he died.

4 Euphemia Ffinch

Euphemia smiled at the three young volunteers approaching from the dormitories.

'Good evening, Euphemia. Hunter tells us the new Warden arrives tomorrow.' The slender girl arched her dark eyebrows. 'It is very soon – almost as if they expected a vacancy.'

The shorter blonde girl said, 'Surely not, Naomi. No-one could have expected poachers would shoot Warden Aiken.'

She looked to Euphemia for support. 'It was a blessing they didn't harm any children.'

'Indeed it was, lass.' She tucked a stray white hair into her straggly bun.

'And that the poachers' truck would not start,' said the tall young man called Hunter, 'or they would have got away before the police arrived.'

'Indeed, they would.'

So much for her tip-off.

'The prisoners say the killer shot at a dragon,' said Naomi. 'It is unlikely to serve them well as a defence.'

'But the children say a great bird flew down before the poacher shot Warden Aiken.' Hunter had questioned the rescued children more thoroughly than the police had.

'The poachers claim the one who escaped killed the Warden,' said Hunter. 'He wore a big straw hat, so the children didn't see his face, and the poachers won't say who he is.'

Euphemia picked up the gilt-edged invitation.

The gang were not poachers but slavers. She had known of Aiken's collusion in arranging the field trip, but the identity of the escaped assassin was a mystery to her too. She listened to the volunteers' theories, fanning herself with the card.

'That looks posh,' said the fair-haired girl, 'like a royal invitation.'

'Right first time, Alice.' She stopped fanning and opened the card, angling it for them to read in the light of the porch's single bulb.

'This is an invitation to the wedding of Princess Aureila of Regalia. I used to be nanny to Princess Aureila and her brother, Prince Alfred.'

She'd expected the Queen to have Alfie married off before his younger sister. Was Alfie the trouble that needed her attention at home? She considered Regalia her home, although she wasn't born there, and had hardly been back since retiring from the palace.

Almost ten years had passed since then. Should she ignore the invitation and return to Djalladin and the Emir?

'Will you come back after the wedding?' asked Naomi.

'Likely not,' she replied. 'I've family matters to see to while I'm in Regalia.'

So, it was a family matter, was it? Not Alfie then. Prince Alfred wasn't family; although it had felt like it sometimes.

'We'll miss you, Phemie. When are you going?'

She calculated. 'Early next week, I think. But you'll be leaving soon yourself.'

'Who will look after the new volunteers?'

'Ach, there'll be someone, lass.' She slipped the invitation into its envelope and stood. 'I'd best go and make my travel arrangements.'

'Good luck with that,' said Alice. 'I couldn't get online at all this afternoon.'

'Ay, well… last time I was here there wasnae any internet.' She picked up the camera. 'I'll leave you three to fight over the comfy chair.'

Sprightlier than she looked, Euphemia hurried through the low wooden building. The people she passed didn't detain her. They didn't seem to notice her.

Her tiny room, tucked behind offices, was conveniently close to the satellite wireless hub which always worked when Euphemia needed it. She flicked the light switch as she closed the door behind her. The dim bulb glowed yellow, illuminating the centre of the bed beneath it and little else.

The light seemed to brighten as she logged in to her laptop and checked her emails, deleting two Facebook notifications and a request for money before opening a message from the private email address of Prince Djarmin of Djalladin.

kestrel@mymail.com

> I regret to inform you that the Emir, our father, died last night.

> It is a shock to us all. Although he still mourned my honoured stepmother, he otherwise seemed well. When I spoke this morning to the Royal Physician, who is away at a conference, he was equally surprised.

> In his absence, a doctor friend of Yu'qub has certified that our father died of natural causes.

> Do you recall your words when you left us? You told me to learn from my father while I could. Who could have known then that I would have so little time to learn from him?

> Although unworthy to fill our father's shoes, I intend to continue with his planned reforms and would value your advice on these when you return to Djalladin.

> My brother and I hope you will attend our father's funeral and my coronation. Where shall we send your invitations?

> Yours Respectfully, Crown Prince Djarmin of Djalladin

She replied at once.

effinch@mymail.com

My condolences to yourself and Yu'qub. I share
your sorrow at your father's untimely death.

He was a good man, who ruled his people well
and would be proud that you continue his
reforms which so many of your statesmen
oppose.

Sadly, family business in Regalia prevents me
from joining you for either ceremony, but my
thoughts will be with you. No doubt, the Royal
Physician – your father's valued friend – will
wish to attend the Emir before His funeral.
Your father may yet have secrets to impart.

You hardly knew your mother before she died.
Your father valued her advice and I believe you
have inherited her commonsense as well as
your father's judgement. Your stepmother was
a worthy successor, but each egg hatches a
different chick. Be careful who you trust.

Yours, Euphemia Ffinch

When Euphemia returned to her inbox, she found a
new email, this time from her goddaughter, Lucinda.

Could this be the family matter needing her
attention? Nothing in the message suggested a
problem. Lucinda – she called herself Cindy on her
email address – had discovered Euphemia's travel
blog and simply emailed to say hello. Lucinda – Cindy

– must be a young woman now, not the child she remembered from Bertie's wedding.

Dear Bertie was always vague about money. His wife had managed their finances until she died when Lucinda was seven years old. Three years after her death, Euphemia was about to retire from the royal nursery when she heard that Bertie was deep in debt.

She'd arranged for a modest windfall to come his way – not big enough to attract attention, but enough to stave off immediate ruin.

She'd told him it was time to overcome his grief, for his daughter's sake, and she'd smartened him up a bit. They'd invited friends he'd lost touch with to Fincham House and settled him back into the world.

Then she went off on her travels.

She'd heard he found himself a wealthy widow and soon after she received a much-forwarded invitation to their wedding.

By the time the invitation reached her there was little time to lose. She left Mexico in a hurry on the day her lodgings burned to the ground.

Fortunately, her hosts were unharmed, having been driving her to the airport at the time. An unmarked police car happened to be passing as the firebombers fled the scene. The police followed them to their hideout and arrested most of the Rodriguez mob: a gang that had terrorised the locality for years.

At the wedding, Bertie's bride was elusive. Lucinda, delighted to see her godmother again, had whisked her away at every opportunity, and there had been little time to get to know the new Baroness, or her three daughters.

Come to think of it, she hadn't heard from Bertie lately.

A shadow troubled her. What kind of godmother was she to lose contact with her goddaughter for so long? Replying to Cindy's email, she described the Emir's palace and the orphanage and asked after cousin Bertie.

Then she booked her flight home for Aureila's wedding.

5 Coming Home

A heaviness settled over Euphemia as she read Lucinda's email, breaking the news that Bertie had died.

The words blurred as she emailed back, asking the lass to give her a video call. Cindy replied that her laptop's webcam didn't work and neither did the microphone. The computer was a cast-off, salvaged from a stepsister's waste bin.

Euphemia's intuition prickled.

Next afternoon she was again online when a call alert sounded.

'Hello, Aunt Phemie. Can you hear me?'

'I can hear ye fine, lass. It's grand to hear your voice. You got your microphone working then?'

'Harriet fixed it for me. She's reinstalled it, but we can't get the webcam to work.'

She remembered Harriet was the youngest stepsister. Maybe her fears were unjustified.

She could sense someone was with Cindy. 'I'm pleased to meet you, Harriet,' she said to the invisible listener, 'and I thank you. You're a good lass.'

Through the laptop came the hollow sound of feet scurrying up wooden stairs.

'You've embarrassed her, Aunt Phee. She's not used to praise. Her mother calls her a beanpole and her sisters are mean to her.'

'They're still living at Fincham House, are they?'

'It belongs to stepmother now. Buttons and I have the basement.'

Of course they did; that's where the kitchen was located. Bertie's old dog was still alive, then.

'Do you spend much time with them?'

'Well… stepmother's allergic to dogs. And I prefer Buttons' company.'

Allergic? She didn't recall any sneezing at the wedding when Buttons had followed the bridesmaids wearing a bow tie.

'Well *my* webcam works fine,' she said, 'and if you click on that little picture of a movie camera you should be able to see me.'

'It works! You haven't changed a bit, Aunt Phemie.'

There were tears in Lucinda's voice. Buttons barked in the background.

'Your picture keeps freezing on the screen, Aunt Phee – can you still hear me?'

'Dinnae fret, hen. I'm coming home. Give my love to Buttons.'

At Regalia's Whittington Airport, passengers were held on board after the plane touched down. A stowaway had been discovered in the baggage hold.

From her window seat, Euphemia watched security guards escort a squat figure from the plane. The poor man was shivering in spite of a blanket from which his head protruded through a hole in the centre. His wide straw hat quivered as two tall officers hauled him across the tarmac, followed by a guard carrying two large knives, a gun, and a long ammunition belt that threatened to trip him.

Eventually, they disembarked, and Euphemia made her way through the busy airport. She was entering a revolving door to exit the terminal when a commotion erupted behind a door marked 'Security'.

Stepping into the nearest taxi, relieved to have avoided another delay, she hardly registered the sirens wailing towards the airport as the taxi drove away.

Her old home in Regalia was now an animal rescue centre, but she'd kept an attic flat above it. After unpacking, she made herself a proper cup of tea, dusted off a table and opened her laptop to check her emails.

kestrel@mymail.com

Thank you, dear friend, for your excellent advice. The Royal Physician has confirmed that my father was poisoned – but you suspected that, did you not?

I have asked him to keep this information to ourselves for a time.

Yu'qub's doctor friend – he who certified our father's death – has lately purchased a yacht and a new Mercedes car.

Those who opposed my father's reforms now court Yu'qub's favour. I do not wish to believe that my half-brother is plotting to supplant me, but I cannot ignore the possibility.

Princess Mona of Carmalay agrees with me that it would be insensitive for us to marry so soon after my father's death. We have postponed our wedding until a more auspicious time.

One of my father's proposed reforms was the inclusion of his daughters in the line of succession. My first act as Emir will be to implement this. Should I then die without an heir, my sister will succeed me as Emira, since she is older than Yu'qub.

If he intends to depose me, this may force him to act quickly, and I will be ready. I cannot detain him without proof. It would send my people the wrong message.

I would that you were here to advise me, as you advised my father. Respectfully, Djarmin.

effinch@mymail.com

You are wise to consider the effect on your people, but be careful, my young friend. Poison is not the only threat.

I cannot yet travel to Djalladin, but I am sure you will judge for yourself when to walk boldly and when to tread carefully.

My good wishes go with you.

Euphemia.

6 Prince Alfred

Aureila's wedding was everything a royal wedding should be: birds twittered, crowds cheered, and cameras flashed. Gift shops ran out of souvenir mugs and tourists mingled with the citizens of Regalia thronging the streets.

At the reception, Prince Alfred sat at the top table, where his sister's smile reflected back at him from every polished silver goblet. Aureila had inherited the natural elegance of their father, the King, and the terrier-like determination of their mother.

Alfred, on the other hand, had all the gentleness of their father and the stature of their mother.

Beside him at the top table sat the bridegroom's sister. 'Your turn next, Your Highness,' she said, and elbowed him in the ribs. Eyes turned towards them. Mothers nudged their daughters and a warm flush crept up from his neck.

'I'm in n-no hurry,' he said.

He was fed up with people telling him it was his turn next. His mother thought it should have been his turn first. But there weren't many princesses around these days, and his mother found objections to any girlfriend he brought home. Not that there had been many of those. Every unmarried girl in the kingdom dreamed of being future queen but, in truth, the daughters of the nobility looked down on him. They were all taller than he was.

Bride and groom left for their honeymoon in a flurry of confetti and rose petals.

The petals came from the bride's bouquet that Aureila threw into the crowd; tradition held that whoever caught it would be the next to marry.

An ungainly young woman elbowed her way through twelve bridesmaids, followed by a plumper lass – Alfred thought their ancestors might have modelled for the gargoyles on the palace roof. He took advantage of the distraction to slip away. Snatches of conversation passed over him as he edged through the crowd.

'Young people today!'

'…them Uglie sisters, Tabitha and Abigail and… what's the other one called?'

Near the side gate, he glanced back through a gap in the crowd, and saw an older woman shove another girl into the brawl.

'I blame it on the TV – all that violence.'

'I blame the parents.'

'That there's their ma in't it? That widow wot married the late Baron.'

'It's gonna take more than catching a bunch o' flowers to marry off them lovelies.'

'…no sign of little Alfred finding 'imself a girl, bless 'im.'

Little Alfred entered a code on the gate's keypad and slipped through, quiet as a mouse. He pulled it shut behind him until he heard the lock click.

Free for the moment, Prince Alfred went to visit the peacocks in the palace gardens.

It was peaceful there. Fountains played, birds sang from the shrubbery and the street clamour was no more than a background murmur, muffled by the thick walls of the palace buildings.

This was one of his favourite places. If no gardeners were about, he would talk to the peacocks. He admired their stately dignity. As a child, he had tried to imitate them, but strutting about with his neck stretched had made him feel silly, rather than stately.

When the peacocks fanned their tails their markings looked like eyes. He felt as if someone was taking notice of him.

Ordinary birds nested in the palace gardens too, and he could identify most of them, but today an unfamiliar visitor pecked among the peacocks. A busy, sparrow-sized bird, it had a black cap and pinkish-red breast, not as bright as a robin's. As he studied it, the bird turned its grey back on him and flew, chirping, to perch in a briar rose.

Alfred beckoned to the Head Gardener.

'What kind of b-bird is that in the b-briar – the one with the pink b-breast?'

'Ah, that be a bullfinch, Highness. And there'll be his missus, come to his call.'

Alfred doubted that. The beige-breasted female was ignoring the antics of the male bird hopping around her. Alfred knew how he felt.

Instead, she flew to the branch nearest Alfred. She dipped her head, as if saluting him, before flying off.

The palace staff were returning from the wedding. He slipped through them and up to his room where he logged into a website for birdwatchers. He posted his sighting.

Alfie: I saw a pair of bullfinches in my garden this afternoon. First time I've seen any in Regalia.

He scrolled down to read the latest comments. When he scrolled back up, a new post had appeared. He didn't recognise the username.

Cindy: A bullfinch sang to me from my basement railings today. Perhaps it was one of yours.

He posted a reply.

Alfie: Are you in Regalia too? You're new to the forum, aren't you?

A moment later a new message appeared.

Cindy: I discovered it today; I haven't had my computer long.

Alfie: I can tell you about some other good websites, but this isn't the best place to chat. Can you Skype or FaceTime?

Cindy: My webcam doesn't work. Neither does the microphone, but we can send messages if you don't mind typing.

He didn't mind typing. His keyboard didn't stammer.

They exchanged usernames and used Skype for their messages. She told him how the laptop had opened her eyes to the rest of the world.

Cindy: I know so little about anywhere outside Regalia. My godmother writes a blog about her travels; she's been everywhere. I'd love to travel the world. I don't even get to leave the house much.

Alfie: Why not?

Cindy: Got to go – someone's calling.

Alfie: Will you–

But she'd logged out.

Next evening, when Prince Alfred logged on to his computer, an alert sounded for a Skype call. It was from Cindy.

He hesitated before accepting it. Could he pretend *his* microphone wasn't working?

He told himself not to be a wimp and began with confidence.

'Hello? Cindy? Can you hear m-me?' (Drat!)

'Hello, Alfie. Harriet got the microphone working for me – she reinstalled it.'

'M-magic! Did she get the webcam working too?'

'She tried, but she couldn't fix it.'

'Try it now, just to make sure.'

But it was hopeless. 'I can see you, Alfie. Can you see me?'

'N-not at all,' he said. 'Just that icon in the m-middle of the screen.' He heard her giggle.

'Never mind,' she said. 'If it started working, Tabitha might want it back. She's already dented her new one.'

She had a clear, musical voice, and she didn't try to finish his sentences for him when he stuttered. Their conversation ended when someone called down to demand tea and toast.

He heard the woman braying, 'Cin-ders?' rising at the end.

Why couldn't *he* sound imperious like that?

7 Catching Up

After the wedding, in festive sunshine Euphemia had watched from the crowd as the Uglie sisters fought over the bridal bouquet.

She remembered them as bridesmaids at Bertie's wedding, where they had ordered around the younger bridesmaids and exchanged furtive sniggers during the service.

As their screeches drew all eyes to the fray, her skin prickled; someone was watching her. Across the crowd, a stocky man wearing a wide-brimmed straw hat looked away as she met his eye.

The man stood as wide as he was tall. In spite of the warm day, he wore a wrap that covered his short body almost to his boots.

His long moustache was streaked with grey. Its mournful droop contrasted with the fierce glitter she glimpsed in his eye before a woman with towering hair pushed in front of him and shoved a lanky girl out into the scrum.

The girl stumbled and almost fell. Her eyes were wide and terrified. If this was Harriet, the youngest sister, then that must be Malegra, their mother.

The vulture-like woman bore little resemblance to Bertie's simpering bride, yet there was something…

Euphemia recalled the hooded eyes that had avoided hers at the wedding.

As the bouquet disintegrated, bridesmaids and guests backed away from flying thorns. Behind the squabble, the moustached man had gone.

As she searched the crowd for him she spotted Prince Alfred, slipping through the onlookers unnoticed, like a mouse through long grass. People were too engrossed in the brawl to notice who was passing under their noses.

He reached a side gate to the palace gardens, entered a key code and was gone.

She didn't need to search the crowd to know Lucinda wasn't there. The old instincts were sharper since her return. Her vision was clearing.

Euphemia visited her friends at the palace in the week after the wedding.

As she'd hoped, the Queen was too busy to spare her much time. Nobody challenged her as she afterwards sought out staff who had been there when she supervised the royal nursery.

That didn't take long either; few still worked at the palace.

Then she was free to seek out Prince Alfred in the palace gardens.

'N-nanny Ffinch – it's so g-good to see you. I still keep all the p-postcards you send, you know.'

She did know. He kept every birthday card as well. With the eagerness of a small child finding someone who will listen, he told her about a new friend – someone he had met online

'We both posted on a b-birdwatching website when we spotted a b-bullfinch – they're rare in Regalia, you know – and since then we've been chatting on Skype m-most evenings.'

'And is she bonnie?'

'I d-don't actually know what she looks like. Her webcam doesn't work. We just t-talk.'

For a rare moment, Euphemia could find no words. Her stillness unsettled Alfie

'Anyway, Nanny, you used to say we shouldn't judge by appearances.' He hesitated. 'She sounds n-nice.'

'Quite right, lad. What did you say her name was?'

'Cindy. Her stepmother calls her Cinders. I hear her shouting orders in the b-background sometimes. Seems to me she's treated like a servant. I'd like to…'

But, being a well brought up prince, he stopped short before recounting what he would like to do.

'I'm sorry, Nanny Ffinch. I've been going on about m-me and haven't even asked how you are? Have you been b-back long?'

'Just for the wedding. I couldnae miss my chick's wedding day, could I now?'

'Are you staying, or will you be off again?'

'I've a family matter to settle first.'

It came out sounding grimmer than she'd intended, and she smiled a reassurance.

'And I cannae miss your birthday, Alfie, can I? Not now I'm here.'

He groaned. 'That b-ball! I'm dreading it. M-mother has invited every titled family with an unmarried d-daughter, and every ex-royal on the p-planet.' Most of the neighbouring countries had sacked their royal families years ago.

He ran a hand through his hair. 'I wish I could invite Cindy, but M-mother would want to know who her family are and who they're related to.'

'Aye, and if you invited her to the Prince's birthday ball, she'd think you were some kind of weirdo.'

Alfred slumped. 'I can't even get away to m-meet her without being flanked by b-bodyguards.'

'If she's a sensible lass she wouldnae agree to meet you alone anyway.'

He sighed. 'I suppose not.'

'Cheer up, laddie. You never know who might turn up on the night.'

'At least you'll be there, Nanny. I'll have someone to t-talk to without worrying about my stammer.'

She didn't have the heart to tell him.

Back home in her flat, Euphemia checked her emails.

kestrel@mymail.com

You knew my brother plotted to kill me too. Did you know how?

Somebody weakened the supports to the palace balcony so I would fall to my death while waving to my people after the coronation.

37

You said I should walk boldly, so instead of waving from the balcony, I decided I would ride through the streets after the coronation to be nearer my people. Yu'qub said this would not be safe or regal and while he argued, his false doctor friend walked out on the balcony. Yu'qub called him back, but he was too late. The weakened beams broke, and the doctor fell to his death.

How did you know?

Humbly yours, Djarmin.

effinch@mymail.com

A wee bird told me.

But, in truth, I didn't know what to expect.

My respects to the new Emir of Djalladin. Honour your father's memory.

Euphemia.

She closed the lid of the laptop and patted it twice, much as she would pat the head of young Alfie all those years ago when he'd pleased her. Collecting bag and cloak, she stepped outside her flat.

The hallway was dark; a light bulb must have gone. The familiar warm animal smell that lingered around the stairwell held traces of... tobacco?

The animal charity might be hosting a visiting dignitary. She would take the lift to the rear exit and avoid any photographers. She pressed the lift button and stepped back to swirl her heavy cloak around her shoulders.

Was that a bump behind her? And a squeal?

The door of the ancient lift squealed open. It must have been that all along, creaking and bumping against the lift shaft.

She entered the lift and pressed the button for the ground floor, looking forward to her next reunion.

8 At Fincham House

Buttons knew Mistress was worried. It was more than a week since she last spoke with Aunt Phemie or had an email from her.

Alterations were complete, and the ballgowns hung in their owners' rooms. The basement seemed bigger without them hanging from chair-backs and picture hooks.

Buttons sensed someone outside before the knock came.

Mistress frowned down at him. 'I paid the milkman this morning, didn't I?'

He ran to the door, his tail wagging, so she opened it. Her godmother swooped in on a breath of cooling afternoon air.

'*What* are you wearing, girl? – Och, I see… your father's shirt.' She enfolded Mistress in her enormous grey cape.

As they hugged, Aunt Phemie's keen eyes ranged over the dingy basement, pausing to wink at him before continuing past to the worn wooden stairs and the cracked window pane halfway up.

She stood back and unfastened the cloak, flinging it over a chair-back. 'You look terrible, hen: pale as porridge. Should you be down here by yourself?'

He barked.

'With Buttons,' she added, bending to rub his ears. 'I'm keeping him company.'

It sounded to him like a perfectly good reason, but Aunt Euphemia raised an eyebrow, and he knew that she understood about staying out of sight, and the Baroness's allergy, and the invitation, and *everything*.

Mistress ended the silence.

'Anyway, they're watching some awful TV reality show up there. I'd rather be here on my laptop.'

'Ay. Well, you dinnae want to believe everything you find on the internet either, lass.'

Aunt Phemie straightened, eyeing the sewing machine on the table, and the laptop opposite. 'How about this lad you've been chatting to online then?'

Mistress stared. 'How–?'

'A wee birdie told me. You know who he is?'

'Yes, but he doesn't know I know.' Her face had flushed the colour of peach blossom.

'We tried a video call. My webcam still doesn't work, but his did. I recognised him from the news.'

Her eyes rested on a stack of newspapers by the fireplace. 'But he's not at all regal.' Would she notice the papers' corners nibbled for a mouse nest? 'He stutters, you know. He seems… unsure of himself.'

'Ach, well. His mother's a mite domineering. And his sister wasn't above giggling at his stutter.'

'Aunt Phemie, how do you know all this?'

'Are you looking forward to the ball tomorrow?'

'Me?'

He barked twice. Aunt Phemie smiled.

'Of course. Every young lass and her family hae an invitation.'

Mistress considered this new possibility. 'They didn't say…'

He barked three times. Cindy frowned down at him, as if hearing his message for the first time.

She shrugged. 'I don't have a ballgown.'

Buttons whined.

Euphemia met his eye and nodded.

'More gumption,' she said.

The girl had lost the will to stand up for herself. Euphemia studied her goddaughter's eyes as if reading the thoughts behind them.

Whoever married the Prince would automatically command respect.

If Alfie fell for her at the ball – and he was halfway there already – her stepmother and stepsisters would have to curtsey to her for the rest of their lives.

So would the rest of Regalia… and the lands beyond.

'Harriet said they ought to take me with them to the ball, and they laughed at her.'

'Harriet stands up for you, does she?'

She watched as Cindy considered this.

'Not really. She can hardly stand up for herself. She's terrified of her mother, and her sisters bully her.'

And now they've you to bully instead, thought Euphemia.

'But you have become friends.'

'She comes down here because I listen and I don't make fun of her. She's grateful that I've altered her dress for the party. She'd look like a model if only she stood straight and put on some airs, like her stepmother. I'm going to do her make-up for her tomorrow.'

'You're not fussed if the Prince notices her then?'

'Oh, he'll notice her. You can't help but notice her; she's a head taller than most people.'

'Does she *want* to be noticed?'

Mistress glanced up the basement stairs. 'Probably not. Except by the Prince, of course; she idolises him.'

'Does she realise how short he is?'

Mistress laughed. 'Like a corgi next to a wolfhound, you mean? Whereas I… am similarly undersized.'

'Petite is the word you're looking for, lass. Your mother was like an elf too. She had some bonny clothes; what happened to them?'

'I've no idea. I don't think Dad would have got rid of them.'

She said, 'Your stepmother will take her daughters to the hairdresser in the morning. Search the attic while they're gone and see what you find. And I'll see what I find.'

She stood and settled her cloak around her shoulders.

'You will go to the ball, Cindy-Ella.'

Pausing at the door, silhouetted by the streetlamp above, she patted her goddaughter's shoulder. 'Sleep well, bairn.'

She turned to mount the basement steps as the door closed behind her.

Her bubbly young goddaughter, overwhelmed by the death of her father and cowed by a malicious stepmother, had lost her spirit.

It was her fault. She was an interfering old woman. Look at that business in Mexico: her friends might have been killed because of her.

All those years ago, she'd interfered and then left them to it.

She had abandoned her cousin to blunder into a disastrous marriage and now young Cindy-Ella was suffering the consequences.

She should have learned by now that being too helpful wasn't the answer. She couldn't just wave a magic wand and make problems disappear. People had to figure things out for themselves, so they'd know what to do next time.

Still, it was only fair that Cindy should have the same chance as everyone else. And if the girl had accidentally given herself a head start over the opposition – good for her!

How much did young Alfie remember of those nursery days, and the things she'd said back then?

kestrel@mymail.com

> After the death of Yu'qub's accomplice, my superstitious people are convinced that his mission was cursed, and I am the rightful Emir.
>
> Yu'qub's followers have abandoned him, many fleeing or going into hiding.
>
> One sold the story of his treachery to the newspapers and now everyone knows of it. My people were ready to lynch him if he appeared on the streets. The traitor is imprisoned, awaiting trial.
>
> My wedding to Princess Mona has been cancelled. I can now admit to my relief at this development.
>
> My intended bride fled Carmalay with her Principal Lady-in-Waiting. Carmalay's Chief Investigator is unable to trace them or uncover any useful leads.
>
> Mona contacted me to apologise for abandoning our alliance. I was able to assure her of my support. Our betrothal was arranged when we were children, and we have met only once since then. We hardly know each other.

She and her companion have changed their names, but I am confident we can rely on your discretion. Should you ever meet Joy Newbold in your travels, please assure her of the good wishes of her former fiancé.

I trust you will not wait on the excuse of a royal wedding to again visit Djalladin and your loyal friend, Djarmin.

9 Preparations

When Buttons jumped on the bed to greet Mistress next morning, she was still asleep. Her eyes, when they opened, shone as bright as they used to before the Master died.

Harriet came down to the basement to help with breakfast.

'They're still being horrible up there,' she said, 'because I told them you should be coming to the ball.'

'Maybe I will,' she said.

Harriet's eyebrows rose. 'One of my gowns might fit you, if you take it up,' but Cindy was laughing. She shook her head, and then the Baroness summoned Harriet from the hall above. It was time to go to the hairdresser.

'Go on,' said Mistress, 'you don't want to be late for the appointment. Come down before you dress for the ball for me to do your make-up.'

The front door opened, and twittering voices entered the house. It closed again as the twittering passed through the hall.

Buttons barked at the stranger coming down their stairs until he recognised Harriet.

'Your hair, it's…' the Mistress paused. 'Actually, it suits you, now I'm over the shock.' Harriet had hesitated but now continued down. 'We can see the shape of your face. It's quite pixy-ish.'

The face under the new haircut had reddened. 'Are you sure you don't mean troll-ish?'

Buttons didn't think so. He'd once watched a TV programme about them with Master and Mistress, and knew that trolls looked like Tabitha.

The make-up didn't take long. With a few strokes, Mistress emphasised Harriet's soft brown eyes and balanced a slight unevenness. Even Buttons saw a difference.

'Magic!' said Harriet. 'My skin's glowing.'

'That isn't make-up. That's you.'

Harriet went to get ready but came down again for their approval before leaving. Mistress had found a russet stole worn in happier times.

'This will set off your ballgown.'

The ceiling creaked as the sisters strutted above, awaiting their taxi.

'Go,' said Mistress. 'Enjoy.'

The stairs creaked too, as Harriet hurried to join them.

As soon as the front door closed, Mistress brought out the ballgown she had found in a trunk of her mother's clothes. It had needed no alteration. She told

Buttons that retro designs were back in fashion as she slipped her feet into her mother's tiny glittering court shoes.

Buttons barked in case she hadn't heard the tapping at the door.

Aunt Phemie bustled in. He ran past her and up the basement steps, to make sure the taxi had left. While he was there the door closed, but it was a warm evening, and he sat watching the cars.

His nose detected a trace of old leather. His eyes followed it to a darker shadow lurking on the neighbour's basement steps. Eyes glinted under a wide-brimmed hat. The shadow moved and a stocky figure stood on the pavement.

'Hello there, feller. You are an old grey one too, is it so? Like old Rodriguez.' As he bent to rub Buttons' ears, the blanket he wore brushed the ground.

'And are you an old scrounger like me, boy? Or do you live here with the young one?' His drooping moustache twisted as he muttered. 'Is she family to that white-haired witch?'

He winced as he straightened. 'I am too old for this. But Rodriguez' brave boys are in prison because of her. My Sofia says they are training for useful occupations.' He spat at the pavement. 'Sofia plans to divorce me and marry the Police Inspector.' He spat again, just missing Buttons. 'That old meddler has taken my family from me so I, Rodriguez, take her family from her.'

A limousine drew up and its driver got out to stand by the passenger door. Under the peaked cap, a sharp little face twitched, and Buttons caught a waft of something familiar. He couldn't quite identify it, his nose confused by competing smells of car exhaust and old leather.

When he turned again, the pavement was empty where Rodriguez had stood, and Mistress was emerging from the basement, transformed.

He might not have known her if he had to rely on his eyes, like humans do.

Her hair shone like polished chestnut as it tumbled around a twinkling tiara. Silver earrings glittered under the streetlights as they trailed like delicate peacock feathers with gems for eye-markings. Even her voice sparkled.

'But I can't just walk through the crowds at the palace gates and up that grand drive.'

Euphemia followed her out. 'A friend of mine will drive you, but he must be back by midnight. Be sure you are ready to leave when he comes for you.'

The gown shimmered, casting an aura of enchantment around the Mistress. When they had found it that morning, in a trunk of her mother's, Buttons didn't recall it looking so… luminous. She lifted its skirts to climb the steps and her shoes flashed like fine crystal.

'Mind now,' called Aunt Phemie. 'Home by midnight.'

The evening was warm, and the vintage limousine was open to the clear summer sky. The purr of its motor was hardly noticeable, although the air was still and the street was now empty.

He caught a waft of jasmine as she passed. Running boards along the sleek, black sides of the limousine served as a step when the chauffeur handed her in.

Buttons blinked.

The sharp-faced driver was behind the steering wheel, the car already moving.

Dogs are good at seeing through disguises, and Buttons smelled a rat. His mistress wasn't going anywhere without him to watch over her.

He ran… and leapt onto the running board.

Too old and too slow, was he?

When the limousine pulled up at the empty palace steps, Buttons jumped off to hide in the bushes.

He heard the car drive away, and a door open above him. Music and voices escaped into the night air before the door closed, leaving only the night sounds of owls and rustling undergrowth.

The Ball promised to be as awful as Alfred had feared. His parents were beside him, greeting the guests. He was only required to say 'P-pleased to m-meet you,' or 'G-glad you could m-make it,' but he thought the reception line would never end. He searched in vain for Nanny Ffinch's comfortable round face among the waiting guests.

Cindy hadn't been online last night. A message on his computer this morning explained that she'd had a visit from her godmother.

But she hadn't been online today either. He'd been up to his room several times to check.

The arriving guests were queuing down the palace steps. He recognised the family inching through the door as the girls who had fought for Aureila's wedding bouquet. They tapped their feet as they waited and jostled the other guests every time the queue moved on. The taller sister was red with embarrassment and hung back from the others, to the annoyance of guests waiting behind. He smiled at her to show he understood.

When they reached the reception line, their mother wouldn't stop talking. The Queen said *three times* that the footmen would take their coats, but they only moved on when the King added, 'Do help yourselves to champagne.'

10 Lady Eleanor

When the last guest was greeted, there was still no sign of Nanny Ffinch. They moved into the reception hall.

The screeches of guests greeting new arrivals assailed his ears and loud 'look-at-me' gowns assaulted his eyes. Steered by his mother to meet potential brides, he struggled to remember the names that went with the glittering tiaras and gleaming teeth.

A footman arrived and stood clearing his throat until the King noticed him.

'The musicians are ready, Sire, whenever Your Highness wishes.'

His Highness raised an eyebrow. The Queen tipped her head a fraction and ended her conversation. She took his arm. The pianist in the corner packed up her sheet music.

Musicians in the ballroom began to play.

The herald announced a late arrival. 'Lady Eleanor of Underwood.'

A crease appeared between the Queen's eyebrows. 'Is that one of the newer states?'

'She has a regal air for one so small,' said the King. 'One of the deposed royals, perhaps?'

The Queen's forehead smoothed. 'That must be it. What an enchanting gown.'

'My dear, it reminds me of the one you wore when we first met.'

'The old fashions are all coming back.'

His parents' conversation faded as he was drawn to the newcomer like a paperclip to a magnet. He hardly noticed the enchanting gown, or the sparkly shoes reflecting the glitter of the chandeliers.

Her eyes were level with his. She smiled as if she knew him and took his arm.

They were together all evening: on the dance floor, at the buffet, around the garden to meet the peacocks, and again on the dance floor. She said to call her Ella.

She didn't try to finish his sentences for him.

He anticipated her likes and dislikes as if they had met before – perhaps in a former life. Even her voice felt comfortably familiar.

Buttons sneaked around the building and found a low wall: wide enough to be comfortable and high enough to see into the ballroom. Mistress was in there with the Prince; her shoes twinkled as they danced. The Prince laughed at something she said, but dogs aren't good at lip-reading. They were well-matched in height and danced easily together. Around the edge of the dance floor, young women gazed with envy in their eyes.

Their mothers looked annoyed.

He couldn't see a ball, anywhere.

The stepsisters sat at a table near his window. Tabitha and Abigail watched the dancers while their mother chatted to a posh-looking gent on the other side of the ballroom. Whenever Harriet rejoined her sisters, her eyes followed the Prince around the room. At least two young men had to repeat themselves before she realised they were talking to her.

Several times during the evening, Prince Alfred spotted his mother heading towards them to cross-examine Ella. As the hours flew past he marvelled that she hadn't reached them yet.

A footman paused with a tray. They each took a glass and he heard his mother's voice behind them.

'…And then some Countess stops me on the way. Or else I have them in my sight, and when I round a pillar, they've gone!'

His father's voice sounded unusually resolute. 'Leave them alone, dear, and come and dance; they're playing our waltz.'

When he turned, his parents were gone – like magic!

He was dancing with Ella when the grand clock in the ballroom began to strike. He glanced at its ornate face with both its hands pointing to twelve, as if turning up its nose at him.

'Midnight already. Doesn't time fly when you're–?'

But Ella had stopped mid-twirl, sending the couples behind swerving to avoid them. She ran from the ballroom.

He followed to the reception hall as she sprinted through the door, past the footmen.

'Stop her! Ella, stop.'

Buttons jumped from his wall and raced to the front of the palace where the limousine stood waiting with its door open. Mistress ran down the steps, stumbling at the bottom.

As the town clock struck its sixth bell, the car began to move.

On the seventh bell, Mistress picked herself up, but the car was gliding away, its door closing. Buttons leapt at the running board, missed by a whisker and rolled sideways into the gutter.

At the eighth stroke, he picked himself up and, ignoring his bruises, raced after Mistress, chasing the limousine. Behind them, a camera flashed, and the Prince called 'Ella' from the palace steps.

The ninth bell tolled.

It was a long driveway.

The last echo of midnight faded as they panted through the gates. There was no sign of the limousine; only an old tin can rattled down the road.

The town clock was still striking when the Prince arrived at the top of the palace steps. A scruffy tan and white mongrel loped down the driveway towards the gates, but there was no sign of Lady Eleanor. Palace staff spilled out of the doorway.

A gleam caught his eye halfway down the steps – surely not a wineglass? Not at a palace ball. A waiter went to retrieve it.

The last stroke of midnight sounded.

The waiter brought him a shoe. It glittered like glass. It was *her* shoe. He called her name again, but only a peacock answered from the gardens.

Among the trees that lined the drive, he thought a shadow moved, but when he ran down to see for himself, there was nobody. A camera flashed.

The steps were filling with people.

He sent palace guards to search the grounds. The Queen said that wouldn't be necessary, but he surprised everyone by insisting.

Buttons limped beside her as she danced home barefoot through the tree-lined streets, swinging a shoe. The gown no longer shimmered. Only the light in her eyes shone, and the moonlight reflecting off the shoe in her hand. She might have been any girl in a long dress on a warm night, humming a dance tune on her way home.

When he glanced back, he fancied he saw a square-shaped shadow moving silently from tree to tree, but when he stopped to look properly he got left behind and had to run to catch up to her.

'Come inside now, Alfred. Your guests won't leave while you're out here.'

Impatience tinged his mother's words, contrasting with the wide smile she aimed at the partygoers lingering in the courtyard. Beside the press van, a reporter spoke into a microphone as guests drifted behind him, pretending not to notice the camera.

'That's a bonnie wee shoe you're holding, laddie.'

'Nanny Ffinch! When d-did you arrive?'

'Oh, a while ago. You were busy.' She fastened the neck of her cloak over a ballgown as blue as a summer lake.

'She's gone, Nanny, and I d-don't know who she is.'

'There can't be many young ladies with a foot that small.'

'I'm going to knock on every door in Regalia until I find her.'

He hadn't stuttered when he said that. For a moment the realisation distracted him. Nanny was smiling, so he knew he was doing something right, until his mother spoke.

'Don't be silly, Alfred; she isn't from Regalia. Your father would have recognised her.'

She was right. His mother was always right, darn it.

'Maybe the lassie's visiting relatives.'

His spirits lifted.

'Even if she leaves Regalia tomorrow, her hosts will tell me where I can find her. I'll ask at every house.'

'You can't personally visit every house, Alfred. It isn't... royal.' His mother forgot to smile at the watching guests. 'And every unmarried girl in Regalia will claim to be this Lady Eleanor. How would you know it was her?'

'I'll know.'

He gazed out across the twittering crowd.

'Nanny Ffinch used to say we would know when we found our one and only true love.'

His mother glared at Nanny Ffinch.

'Ay. Well... I expect we were talking about fairy tales, your Highness.'

'And there I was, thinking someone else...' For a moment, he looked uncertain.

'Such a dinky wee shoe.'

He raised the glittering shoe Nanny Ffinch was admiring. As it caught the glow of a lamp above the palace door, reflected light flashed across the courtyard – yellow and silver and rose gold – causing spectators to gasp.

He knew what he must do.

As he followed his mother into the palace he said, 'They'll all have to try on the shoe. Nanny's right. There can't be many who could wear it.'

He turned to Nanny Ffinch for support, but she had gone.

11 After the Ball

Aunt Phemie was waiting by the gate to the basement steps.

'I'm so sorry, Aunt Phee. I forgot the time.'

Buttons followed Mistress down the steps. At the door she turned, and he nearly bumped into her.

'I ran like anything when I heard the clock strike, but the car was already driving away and I stumbled on the steps. I'm afraid I've lost a shoe.'

She opened the door and dropped the other shoe on the doormat. He went in to drink from his water bowl; it had been a long evening.

He heard his name and listened again.

'Buttons tried to stop the car, and we ran after it but by the time we got to the gates it had disappeared.' She held the door open. 'Are you coming in?'

'How was Prince Alfred?'

'He's sweet. He doesn't stutter so much once he's relaxed. We danced every dance. I'm sure I could learn to love him.' She cocked her head, considering. 'He's actually rather good-looking. I can see why Harriet's smitten. Poor Harriet.'

She turned fully to face her godmother.

'What's it like, to be that crazy about someone?'

'You may never know if you marry Alfred.'

Her tone had hardly altered, but Buttons heard the change. Aunt Phemie was listening differently.

'But, Aunt Phee, I'd get to travel the world and see all the places you've seen.'

'Not the places I've seen, lass.' She came down the steps to the door. 'You'd see a lot of airports and security screens and hotel suites. You'd see the orphanages and hospitals when they've been stood to attention for a royal visit – not their everyday faces.'

Mistress leaned against the doorpost.

'It must feel good to help people, like you do.'

'Och, I'm getting too old to be much help. It's young people who do all the work. I just show around the volunteers who come for a couple of months, sometimes after they've left college or before they go. There are companies that arrange it all and send them over.'

'Could I do that, do you think?'

Aunt Phemie acknowledged the possibility with a tilt of her head.

'Or you could come with me.'

Buttons nuzzled his Mistress's leg to remind her he was there.

Cold air blew through the doorway; a night breeze was stiffening.

'I'm off now, lass. We'll meet again before I go.'

For once, Buttons was glad to see her leave.

Mistress closed the door and turned on the radio.

Buttons ran up the stairs to a small window that helped light the staircase during the day. This was where he would watch for Mistress's return when she went shopping and bark at cats who skulked under parked cars.

While Mistress went through to the bedroom, he watched Aunt Phemie mount the steps.

A movement at the street corner drew his attention. A squarish figure in a wide-brimmed hat stepped into the road and aimed something long at Aunt Phemie. Was it a wizard's staff? His hat wasn't very tall, but it *was* sort of pointy.

The staff must be heavy since the wizard needed both hands to raise it to his shoulder and aim it. Buttons barked to warn Aunt Phemie.

As she turned, a spell whizzed past her head, parting stray hairs that had escaped her bun. Something invisible thudded at the door.

The wizard raised his staff again and aimed as a taxi rounded the corner and knocked him down.

The driver managed to stop the cab before its wheels ran over him. Or maybe the wizard stopped it with a magic spell.

Scrambling to his feet, the man stumbled away. He merged into the shadows between houses, and Buttons lost sight of him.

Unaware of the excitement in the street, Cindy returned to the kitchen in pyjamas as a newsreader reported the flight of Lady Eleanor of Underwood from the royal ball.

She turned up the radio to listen. The Prince had vowed to search every home in Regalia for the mystery guest who lost a shoe while fleeing the palace.

Upstairs, the front door crashed open.

The Baroness and her girls flocked into the hallway, still exclaiming over the rapid recovery of the man who their taxi had knocked down.

Harriet flew down the stairs.

'Oh, Cindy, the Prince smiled at me!' Her hands clasped at her chest.

'But then this Lady Eleanor turned up – nobody knew who she was – and Prince Alfred didn't dance with anyone else all night. They were together the whole time.

'Then, at midnight, she ran out of the palace and disappeared. The Prince didn't come back to the ball after that, so everyone went home.

'We hung around for *ages* waiting for a taxi, but I didn't care. I was happy watching the Prince. *I* wouldn't run away from him, ever. He was so masterful. He sent the palace guards to search the grounds in case she'd fallen into the lake or something, and he wouldn't let go of the shoe he'd found on the steps, and he told the guard captain that tomorrow they would start searching every…

'home…

'in the…'

Mouth open, she stared at the doormat.

The shoe Mistress had left there sparkled in the light from the naked bulb above.

Buttons jumped up at Harriet to divert her attention, but by then Tabitha had appeared at the top of the stairs to demand hot chocolate. The shoe twinkled, and her shriek brought their mother.

The Baroness speared it with her eyes.

Her gaze remained fixed on it as she came down the stairs, as if it might scuttle off if she looked away. She picked it up carefully, like an animal that could bite. Only then did she turn to Mistress in wonder.

'You!

'It was you.'

After that Buttons had to fend for himself – they all did without Mistress to run around after them.

They'd tried to catch him too. Malegra had blocked the stairs while Tabitha and Abigail made to head him off before the dog flap, but clumsy Harriet got in the way and he escaped between her lanky legs.

The garden door was locked, and nobody bothered to find the key to follow him, so he crept back to listen behind the door.

Dogs have good hearing. He heard the Baroness announce that Cindy must be kept out of sight while the Prince was searching his kingdom for her.

He heard Tabitha screech when she spotted her old laptop on the table. After smashing that up, she followed her mother and sisters upstairs, complaining all the way, and their voices grew muffled until they were lost behind the drawing-room door.

He waited a while longer before creeping back through the dog flap.

Mistress stirred in the under-stairs cupboard and he whined softly at the door.

'Shh, Buttons. Don't let them hear you. While I'm locked in here, I can't protect you if she catches you.'

This was a new thought to Buttons. Wasn't he the one doing the protecting? Shouldn't that be how it worked?

Over the next days, he ate from scraps he found on the washing-up which piled up on the draining board. And the dresser. And the table. They were all terrible cooks, so there were plenty of scraps.

The mice ate well too. He hadn't the heart to chase them.

Malegra kept the key to the cupboard on a cord around her neck and only gave it to Abigail when it was time to take Mistress her meals and empty her bucket.

At night, when everyone slept, Harriet crept down and whispered to Mistress through the door. Buttons thought Harriet looked ill. He hadn't seen her eat since the night of the ball.

When the TV news was on, he crept up to listen at the door. But the press soon lost interest, and updates on the Prince's search for the mystery woman were reduced to a final comment before the weather report.

12 Alfie's Quest

For almost a week, a gaggle of reporters and TV cameras had covered the Prince's search for the woman who left her dainty shoe on the palace steps.

By the second week, a single cub reporter still followed the hunt, in hope of an exclusive scoop.

The palace Press Officer told Alfred that this was the son of the newspaper's owner, so nobody complained about his prolonged absence from the newsroom.

Another day, another street, and the Prince's team arrived at yet another front door.

This one belonged to a grand house on the corner of an elegant street. Curtains stirred as they approached. Alfred heard scurryings inside as they mounted the steps to the front door.

An attendant pounded the heavy knocker.

In the silence that followed, the door creaked open and a tall woman peered out. She redirected her gaze downward, and the door opened wider. She curtseyed, while three ungainly young ladies bobbed in the hallway behind her.

He almost said, 'Sorry, wrong house.' But everyone knew why he was there, and he didn't like hurting people's feelings.

An attendant handed him the shoe, and he repeated his line about looking for its owner. The older woman curtseyed again and produced another exactly like it, only for the other foot.

'It belongs to my daughter, Your Highness.' She gestured towards the three giants behind her. 'This is its pair.'

For a frantic moment, Alfred wondered if someone could have slipped an enchantment into his drink at the ball. A camera flashed behind him.

Buttons looked on from the stairwell's shadows as the Baroness claimed the sparkling shoe was her daughter's.

The Prince looked from one to another as the sisters continued bobbing like plastic ducks in a bath. Behind him the camera flashed again, and one courtier smiled at something another one said. Buttons thought he'd asked what the Prince had been drinking at the ball, but dogs aren't good at lip-reading.

'Are these *all* your daughters?'

The Baroness simpered. 'Indeed, Your Highness, all three are my chicks.'

'Actually, I meant…'

The Prince cleared his throat.

'P-procedure must be observed. Whose foot fits this shoe?'

Buttons had watched the Baroness struggling to push her great claw into the shoe she now held. She wouldn't lose face by trying the one the Prince offered. She left its twin on a chair and pushed Tabitha forward.

Tabitha's foot hung over the back of the Prince's shoe.

Abigail's bulged over the sides.

Harriet shook her head, but her mother pushed the shoe over her toes so hard they bled. When Harriet whimpered, Malegra pulled it free with a curse and threw it at the wall where it shattered into slivers of bloodied crystal and stardust.

Buttons darted forward and seized the other shoe from the chair. He ran with it down the basement stairs while the Baroness thundered, 'Leave! Bad dog. Bu-tt-o-ns,' her voice sharpening to a point.

The Prince followed him down, and the Baroness blustered after them.

Alfred heard the dreadful woman protesting behind him and shuddered at the thought of her as a mother-in-law. He remembered her now from the reception line at the ball. And her daughters – what were their names?

The dog dropped the shoe in front of a cupboard door and barked. Hadn't she called him Buttons?

Someone answered from inside the cupboard.

The tallest sister ran down the stairs. 'Cindy, the Prince is here. It's going to be alright.'

Cindy? He looked down at the dog.

Buttons.

He tried the door handle, but the cupboard was locked. He couldn't trust his voice, so he held out his hand for the key and let his face tell them what he thought of them. The old witch backed away.

'UNLOCK THIS DOOR.'

It didn't sound like him. For the first time in his life, he sounded like someone who expected to be obeyed.

He tried it again.

'NOW! …please.'

The tall one – Harriet, that was her name – came forward with a large pair of scissors and lunged at her mother. What further crimes were these people capable of?

Harriet's dark eyes flashed as she snipped a cord around her mother's neck and caught the key that fell from it. But she trembled as she held it out to him.

When their hands touched, she flinched as if burned.

Lady Eleanor emerged from the cupboard. Her hair was tangled, and her pyjamas covered in coal dust, but she was his Ella. And, it appeared, his Cindy too. Something inside him relaxed. Everything was as it should be.

She didn't seem surprised to see him.

Her foot slipped easily into the shoe Buttons had dropped.

'So,' he said, 'this is Buttons. Pleased to meet you, Buttons. I'm Alfie.'

How long had Cindy known who he was?

He recalled their one-sided video call. Deciding to think about this later, he lowered himself to one knee.

The two older stepsisters watched from the stairs. The reporter elbowed his way between them, and his camera flashed.

Without a stutter Prince Alfred said, 'Cindy… Lady Eleanor… whoever you are, will you marry me?'

13 All the Time in the World

Silent tears trailed down Harriet's face. The camera flashed again, and Buttons wondered how the palace dogs would welcome a terrier of uncertain family.

Mistress's voice was steady. 'Dear Alfie… I'll always treasure our friendship, and our magical evening at the ball, but I'm not ready to marry yet. I want to travel the world with Aunt Phemie.'

'Oh!' Harriet's hand covered her mouth.

Buttons whined. Fincham House without his Mistress was an even worse prospect than the palace dogs.

The Prince backed into a chair and sat, speechless. The camera flashed again.

'Y-your Highness.' Harriet curtseyed. 'Cindy, can I suggest the privacy of the study?'

'Good thinking, Harriet,' said Mistress. 'Tabitha, could you bring us up some tea please?'

Everyone stood back as Mistress swept up the stairs, followed by the Prince and Buttons, who slipped into the study behind them. When Master was alive, the study had been their favourite room.

They all agreed the tea tasted awful.

On his way out, the Prince invited Mistress to the palace. Buttons approved. With a better idea of what she was turning down, Mistress might change her mind.

The Baroness declared it was an excellent idea and she would accompany her stepdaughter as chaperone. But when the time came, Mistress took Harriet instead.

Their visits became a regular event.

The basement was lonely without them.

'I'm pleased Alfie's given up trying to change my mind,' said Mistress one afternoon on their return. 'He seems more settled since Aunt Phee's visit to the palace last week.' She went to fill the kettle.

Harriet paused before replying.

'He's asked if I'll still visit him, after you're gone.' Her face looked hot. 'Do you mind?'

'Mind? I'm delighted,' said Mistress, turning on the tap. 'I can tell he likes you.'

Harriet drooped. 'If only I weren't so tall.'

'A queenly height.'

'But it's you he wanted.'

Mistress turned off the tap and paused. 'I don't think that matters.' She set the kettle on its base and flipped the switch.

'It takes two, after all. Aunt Phee says it's like birds' eggs.'

'Um… I don't know much about birds. Although Alfie's teaching me.'

Mistress came to sit beside Harriet, and Buttons settled at her feet.

'A hen bird can lay an egg without a mate, but it won't hatch.' She bent to rub Buttons' ears. 'It takes two birds to make an egg that will grow a chick.'

'Oh. I see what you mean.'

Buttons didn't, but Harriet sounded happier.

Mistress nodded. 'And it takes two to grow a relationship.'

The kettle turned itself off and she went to make tea. As she brought two mugs to the table, Harriet said, 'What will you do about Buttons?'

He cocked an ear for her reply, but their voices were low, and dogs aren't good at lip-reading.

So, Mistress still planned to leave Regalia.

He resolved to run away, but Mistress had other plans.

She took him to the vet.

Buttons trembled in the waiting room. A cat hissed at him from its travel cage, but he was too worried to bark at it.

Mistress tried to cheer him up with a dog biscuit. After a moment's hesitation he took it, just as they were called in for their appointment.

The vet waited while he ate it. 'What a lucky dog,' she said. 'It must be your birthday.'

And then she stuck a needle in him.

If that was what happened on your birthday, Buttons didn't want another one.

If he ever got out of there, he was going to run away.

But the vet said, 'When you bring him for his second vaccination, I can sign his passport form. Then you can complete his travel arrangements.'

And Buttons understood.

They were taking him too. Travelling the world with Mistress and Aunt Phemie would be one long birthday treat.

It was Euphemia who picked up Buttons' new passport and delivered it to Fincham House. She presented herself at the front door this time.

Buttons panted up the stairs, to arrive as Baroness Malegra was grandly declaring that her youngest daughters were at the palace. Euphemia said they would be back soon, and she would wait.

She settled herself on a chair in the entrance hall and complimented Malegra's hairstyle. The Baroness nodded graciously before she was seized by a sudden fit of sneezing and excused herself to find a tissue.

As Malegra disappeared upstairs, Euphemia sat forward in the chair to stroke him, but sudden pounding at the front door set him growling.

'What is it, boy? Who's out there?'

She went to open the door, standing behind the thick oak as she pulled. Something whizzed past and a picture frame shattered on the opposite wall.

Buttons leapt to the doorway. A short, stocky man with a droopy moustache stood on the doorstep. Eyes glittered under a large sombrero. The man adjusted his raised arm to point a long pistol at Aunt Phemie peeping around the door.

'You won't escape Rodriguez this time.'

Buttons launched, sinking sharp teeth into the gunman's leg. Man and dog tumbled down the front steps of Fincham House and another shot rang out.

Splinters flew from the door frame.

He released the leg and the man grabbed it with his free hand, rolling around the pavement and whimpering in pain as Buttons darted in and out, nipping where he could.

Aunt Phemie watched from the doorway. 'Good dog, Buttons. Go for it, boy.'

The gunman waved his gun at Buttons and fired. A lamp above the door exploded.

He aimed the pistol again as a car bearing the royal crest pulled up at the kerb. A bullet bounced off the toughened glass of the royal limousine, leaving a spider-shaped crack.

The gunman scrambled to his feet and limped away as fast as he could drag his injured leg. The security guard who'd accompanied Cindy and Harriet home overtook him easily.

Mistress examined him from head to tail to make sure he had no bullet wounds. Everyone made a fuss of him.

After the Mexican was taken for interrogation and the royal limousine returned to the palace, Harriet made them tea and toast in the basement with extra toast for Buttons.

Slowly, his heartbeat returned to normal as voices chatted above him.

'Thanks for picking up his passport, Aunt Phee. Now I'll have more time to pack this afternoon.' She added the envelope to a pile of papers on the table. 'Did Harriet tell you? Alfie has asked her to carry on visiting him after we're gone.'

Harriet blushed crimson and looked at her feet.

'I just wish I weren't such a beanpole.'

Aunt Phemie shook her head and tutted.

'I'm sorry, lass, I havenae a magic wand to shrink you. And there are no magic beans to make Alfie grow either.'

Harriet protested. 'Oh, I don't mind that he's short.'

'So why should he mind that you're tall?'

Harriet raised her eyes to meet Aunt Phemie's.

'Be your own self, lass. If you changed, you'd be someone else. He might not like that person so well. Would ye want to risk it?'

Harriet straightened as she considered this.

Mistress said, 'After next week you'll have him all to yourself. Where are we going first, Aunt Phee?'

'There's nae rush, lass.

'We can mosey across the continent first and maybe pick up a sea crossing. We'll make a sea-dog of old Buttons, shall we?'

She bent to rub his ears.

'Or we might fly down and drop in on some friends of mine in Tanzania. You'll like it there, boy; lots of new smells.

'Then we could pop across and visit young Djarmin, who I'd like you to meet but he's a mite busy right now.

'So there's nae rush.'

Happy Ever After

They all lived happily ever after.

Well, most of them.

Rodrigo Rodriguez was convicted of attacking the royal limousine and attempting to assassinate a member of the Regalian royal family. On his eventual release, he would be returned to Mexico, where he was wanted for crimes committed there.

After the judge announced his sentence, the prisoner declared he would use his time behind bars to write the history of the infamous Rodriguez gang.

On his way out of court, he was overheard telling the guard how he would enjoy learning to read and write.

Tabitha and Abigail helped the cub reporter write his story and subsequently landed jobs at the newspaper.

As fashion editor, Tabitha got to order people around, which made her happy and, strangely, less bossy.

Abigail became famous as Aunt Abby, answering readers' letters. She married the reporter and they had a son called Jack – but that's another story.

At the wedding of Prince Alfred and Harriet Uglie, the mother of the bride was seized by a sneezing fit at the wedding banquet. Her final sneeze was so violent it dislodged her elaborate hairstyle, which slid majestically sideways.

Newspapers and newsreels around the world featured photographs of Baroness Malegra, mother of the future Queen, with her wig hanging from an earring while flashlights reflected off a head as shiny as Humpty Dumpty's.

If you enjoyed this book
please leave a review on Amazon

About the Author

Cathy Cade is a former librarian who began writing in retirement. She lives with her husband and dogs, mostly in Cambridgeshire's Fenland and occasionally in a suburb of London, across the fence from Epping Forest.

Cathy's writing has been published in *Scribble*, *Best of British, Tales From the Forest,* and *Flash Fiction* magazines, and *To Hull and Back Short Story Anthology 2018*, as well as in collections from the Whittlesey Wordsmiths: *Where the Wild Winds Blow* and *A Following Wind.* Her books, *Witch Way, and other ambiguous stories* and *A Year Before Christmas* are available from Amazon and Smashwords.

Find Cathy online at www.cathy-cade.com.

Other Books by Cathy

Witch Way
and other ambiguous stories

Cathy Cade

Sixteen stories, some placed or shortlisted in competitions.
Add a flash or two, some verse, and a motley collection
of characters who aren't all they seem – or are they?
You decide.

Meet mirlings and brownies, a citizen of Pompeii,
an unsettled soul, a misguided confidante,
an unlikely Samaritan, a trainee mortician, and a witch...
or not.

From Goodreads: *'Have reread it several times'*; from
Amazon: *'A little gem of a collection'*; *'had me on the edge of my
seat … Definitely worth a read'*; from Sally Cronin: *'An eclectic
collection … varied and entertaining'*.

A Year
Before Christmas

by

Cathy Cade

Emmie the Elf works hard, running errands and sweeping out
reindeer stalls, but Santa's newest helper still finds herself grounded
on the biggest night of the year.
Can Emmie get airborne in time for next Christmas Eve?

Available from Amazon and Smashwords

FROM THE WHITTLESEY WORDSMITHS

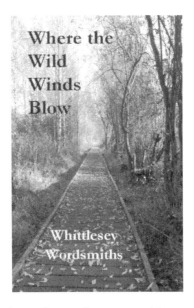

Stories and verse from our writing group
Available from Amazon

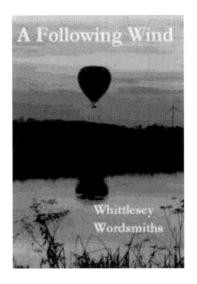

MEMOIR OF A FEN CHILDHOOD

IN AN UNUSUAL HOME

The Railway
Carriage Child

Wendy
Fletcher

Available from Amazon

Printed in Poland
by Amazon Fulfillment
Poland Sp. z o.o., Wrocław

63830274R00054